Jonathan branch is the American author of some of American favorite short self-published children's books. He began writing poetry and teaching Pre algebra at the age of 18. He is a celebrated and established author and awarded writer by many. His book shows display his works at Barnes and noble, local book stores and toy stores in Princeton, New Jersey and in Hopewell, Virginia. Jonathan branch is a former firefighter and rescue squad member. He is also up for the African American world record for the title of most children's books. He speaks 3 languages and teaches GED courses online for displaced individuals who look up to him for guidance. He has spoken on the radio and has given many speeches all over the states. He has received numerous awards including the prudential youth leadership award, awards from Washington dc and was the former vice president of toast masters. Currently he is working on medical patents for children with physical therapy and bone cancer equipment for pediatric patients.

Welcome to Childbranch Books

We have written the best action and adventure books for children for years. So sit back and get ready to travel far away to rescue a princess or fight a dragon ....

Enjoy the magic ....

To all the parents that love to read our books at night to your lovely children.....

Thank You

We will continue our great work in pursiut of great accomplishments. Our illustrators are from Italy, London and the Philippines. We have 235 books to write so keep reading ......

Timmy woke up to a cold winter morning. The snow was still on the ground. His dad was leaving early to plow snow.

The clock chimed 10.
Timmy's dad was late.

He grabbed his boots and
ran out the door. He left
his coffee mug on the
countertop.

Timmy looked out the window as the snow began to fall.

The plow was outside and the heat was on.

Timmy sat at the end of the table looking at all the food that came out of the oven.

There were vegetables,
cupcakes, brownies,
macaroni, and sweet and
spicy chicken.

The snow was 12 inches thick.
Good enough to make snow angels.

Whoooooooosh! Sam threw a snowball at Timmy.

As it whizzed past his head, Timmy threw one back and got Sam right in the nose. "You throw like a girl," yelled Timmy.

Splat! Timmy and Sam both got hit by snowballs thrown by Ashley.

Timmy went inside, since it was getting colder. His mother was making strawberry cupcakes.

FLOUR

Once the cupcakes were put in the oven, they had to wait.

Timmy walked outside next to the snowman. It was lonely in the house. It was quiet and there was no one to play with.

Timmy picked up snow in his hand and made it into a ball. He threw it at the snowman.

The snowman's hat fell off into the snow.

"Why so sad?" asked the snowman.

"My Dad's not here, he's working and there's nothing to do.

I'm so bored," yelled Timmy.

"All my friends
are gone and
everyone left
me."

"Let's see what everyone else is doing," said the snowman. They walked across the street and saw a family in front of the fireplace warm and happy.

Timmy walked home and made a wish. He heard a noise behind him. A man was walking up the walkway with a snowplow parked on the curb.

Timmy's wish had come true. "Dad, what happened at work?" he asked.

"They gave me a day off. James will do the block for me. I'm tired." Timmy and Dad raced in the house from the cold.

"So Timmy, what do you want the do, sit in front of the fireplace?"

"No," said Timmy.
"Every boy needs his 7
hours of TV. Grab
some popcorn."

His Dad and Mom looked at each other and realized he might be watching a bit too much TV.

We would like to take the time to thank our amazing illustrators and editors

Edward Kos

Raymond Ariola

Amy foster

Clizia Brozzesi

Jhoiye Mendoza

Michele Paoluccci

Raymond Ariola passed away during the philippines storm. We will miss him greatly!

More Spectacular Books on the Way !!

Made in the USA
Middletown, DE
07 June 2019